BY ALISON HENDRIE
BASED UPON THE SCREENPLAY BY
DAVID MICKEY EVANS AND ROBERT GUNTER

Published by The Trumpet Club
1540 Broadway, New York, New York 10036

TM & © 1993 Twentieth Century Fox Film Corporation.
All Rights Reserved.

No part of this book may be reproduced or transmitted in any form or by
any means, electronic or mechanical, including photocopying, recording
or by any information storage and retrieval system, without the written
permission of the Publisher, except where permitted by law.

ISBN: 0-440-40911-X

Produced by Neuwirth and Associates
Printed in the United States of America
May 1993

3 5 7 9 8 6 4 2
OPM

A loud *SMACK* filled the schoolyard as the baseball connected with the catcher's mitt.

"Steerike!" yelled the catcher as he threw the ball back to the pitcher's mound.

At the plate, Benny Rodriguez stared straight ahead, never taking his eyes off the pitcher. He leaned slightly forward, pulled the heavy wooden bat to his shoulder, and waited for the next pitch.

"Take that, ya bums!" called Benny as he hit the ball clear across the playground, deep into right field.

As he ran around the bases, Benny could hear his buddies cheering him on. He loved baseball.

Benny was fast, probably the fastest kid in school. He was also one of the coolest. When Benny spoke, everybody listened—even the teachers. He wasn't much taller than the other guys, but somehow he seemed bigger. His brown hair would flop over his big brown eyes when he played ball. And that was just about all Benny ever wanted to do.

Quick feet kicking up gravel as he rounded second base easily, Benny passed third with no problem. He was on his way home.

Suddenly, the ball arced toward home plate. What could he do? If he went to home, he'd be tagged out. If he ran back to third, the ball would be thrown to the base, and he'd be out there, too.

But Benny just smiled. His own team—a group of guys who

played baseball together every day—were rooting him on from the sidelines.

"Pickle, Benny, pickle," screamed "Ham" Porter, hanging on to the backstop fence until his knuckles turned white.

Ham was a chubby kid, always eating a candy bar or a doughnut. He was also always smiling. Ham could find the fun in just about anything.

"You got it, man! Come on home! Look at him rubba-legging!" yelled Kenny DeNunez, laughing at the way Benny was faking out the other team by moving all over the place.

Kenny was as skinny as Ham was fat. He was a handsome kid who looked like a scarecrow when he ran, but he was smooth and sure when he pitched for Benny's team.

"He moves right, he moves left. Rodriguez is the king of the pickle, ladeees and gennlemen!" said Bertram Grover Weeks, imitating a sports announcer.

Bertram didn't really have a nickname, although some of the kids called him "four-eyes" because of his thick, horn-rimmed glasses. No one ever called him that in front of Benny, though.

Cries and chants were ringing out from behind the chain-link fence where Benny's teammates—also his best friends—were standing. The gang was going wild, screaming advice to their star player.

Benny faked right, then left, pulled the old "rubba-leg" move that the pros do so well, making it look as if he were running in two different directions at once. The catcher threw the ball to third, still trying to get Benny tagged out. That was all Benny needed: with lightning speed, he raced down the baseline and crossed home plate as whoops of joy greeted him on the other side. He had scored the winning run.

Squints Palledorous, a short, wise-guy of a kid who always had his radio plugged into his ear—even in school—suddenly yanked the plug out and shouted over all the noise.

"Hey! Wills stole another one! Maury Wills just stole his

thirty-first base!" he cried with a lopsided grin spreading over his lightly freckled face.

Maury Wills, a famous baseball player, was an idol of Benny's. And because Benny was kind of the leader, Wills was a hero to all the other guys, too.

"All right!"

"Oh, cool. I wonder when he'll break the record?"

"He is *so* hot this year, man, he's gotta be made MVP."

The guys slapped each other on the backs and started heading back toward the school.

Across the playground, the other team wasn't so happy. They were all blaming one another for losing the game.

"Ya lousy dufes," someone moaned. "How could you let the guy get into a pickle?"

"Yeah, you know he's got truly rubba legs," said another.

"That's it, man, we gotta get Benny on our team next time," said the first guy, throwing his baseball glove on the ground.

Still laughing and shoving each other, Benny, Squints, and the rest of the gang chomped on huge wads of Bazooka bubble gum and spit loudly and messily onto the playground.

"Yes!" shouted Squints. "Murderers' Row reigns!"

"Yeah-yeah," added Alan "Yeah-Yeah" McClennan. "Sixteen to zippo. Undefeated!"

Yeah-Yeah jumped around the team, slapping backs and giving high fives. The kid was always moving, as though he had ants in his pants. He started every sentence with "yeah-yeah," so it was easy to pick a nickname for him.

The lunchbell rang, calling all the ballplayers back to reality. The other team couldn't resist one last dig.

"Awwh, ya muthas wear boxer shorts!"

"Yeah, when's the last time yours shaved her mustache?"

Laughing loudly and shoving each other, exchanging stupid insults, the kids went back to class. The playground was quiet and empty. Except for one kid.

Me. Scotty Smalls. Straight-A student, short, serious. And new at school. I stood back, feeling a little nervous around the crowd and feeling very left out. It was 1962, and I was in the fifth grade. I had just moved into town. I didn't know anybody. And now summer vacation was one day away and I didn't have a chance to meet anybody.

Kicking a pebble as I started toward the door, I was feeling sorry for myself. New town. New neighborhood. No friends. And now—three whole months of vacation with no one to hang around with. What was I going to do all summer?

As I entered the redbrick schoolhouse, I noticed a commotion at the water fountain.

Benny, Ham, Yeah-Yeah, and Squints were elbowing each other next to three water fountains along the far wall. I could barely hear what they were saying, but it sure sounded like fun. I watched their easygoing play with envy. I really wanted to have friends like that.

"Milk!" shouted Yeah-Yeah as he pointed to one of the three fountains.

"Oh, man!" cried Ham. "I'm dyin' of thirst! Whaddya doin' to me?"

I was still too far away to hear the game. I could hear him say "milk" okay, but what was the other word? Sounded like "pee" to me. I moved closer.

"Ah, you big baby," Squints chuckled, loudly slurping up his drink out of one of the fountains.

"C'mon, Ham, it ain't really pee," said Benny, trying hard not to laugh as he drank fast and noisily from the other "milk" fountain.

"Oh, yeah? Then why don't you switch with me?" asked Ham.

"What, you think I'm stupid or something?" said Benny, this time laughing out loud. He fake-punched Ham and moved out of his friend's way so Ham could have a drink too.

Oh, now I got it. Squints had "cursed out" one of the

fountains, saying it was pee. Now I knew how I could join the game. All I had to do was drink out of the milk fountain. Because, after all, no one would drink out of the pee fountain.

No one, that is, except the new kid in town.

"Boy, am I thirsty," I said, trying to sound cool as I walked across the hall.

The guys were nudging each other and looking at me with interest. I walked right up to what I thought was the milk fountain, flashing a smile at my soon-to-be friends. They still laughed. Was my fly open or something? I had been too far away to see which one Squints called "pee." So I just had to guess.

I guessed wrong.

"Uggh! Gasp, I'm gonna be sick!" squealed Ham. "He's drinking pee!"

"Barf!" said Squints, clutching his throat.

"Aw, there goes my lunch," added Benny, doubling over and grabbing his stomach.

At this, my head jerked up, making me smack my ear against the heavy tile fountain. I saw stars for a good five seconds.

The guys were holding their throats now, laughing and making gag sounds. A couple of them pretended to barf all over the floor until they could hardly stand up. They moved down the hall, cracking up so hard that they were almost falling down. Well, at least I'd made an impression. But I hadn't made any friends.

A few hours later, the final bell of the school year rang. Even though the halls were now jammed with cheering fifth graders out for summer vacation, I wasn't very excited.

"Excuse me...ouch," I said as the students began moving fast toward the door.

"Hey, watch it." I was being bounced and pushed from one kid to the next.

"Sorry."

"Outta the way!"

"Move it, shrimp."

As I tried to go down the stairs, I was suddenly lifted off my feet by the crowd. Moving together as if we were one giant caterpillar, we went down the stairs and headed outside.

It was a little easier to see now that I was off the ground. As I tried to figure out just where I was, I noticed Benny and his gang walking down the street. I had to get out of this crowd.

My feet hit the ground and, struggling and shoving, I pushed my way through the screaming kids. At last, I was free!

I tailed the guys through the neighborhood, making sure they didn't see me. And then they disappeared.

"Hey, you loser, over here!" I heard someone yell. When I turned in the direction of the voices, no one was there.

"Ha ha! Did you see that?" someone else shouted, this time closer. How could they see me if I couldn't see them?

I peeked through a bunch of trees. On the other side of a fence was the biggest, crummiest-looking playground I had ever seen.

As I snuck through the fence, I saw the gang joking and laughing with one another. They hadn't been talking to me. They didn't even know I was there.

"No more school," shouted Squints, tossing something to Ham.

"No more teachers, no more books," chanted Ham, catching the thing—a tool, I thought—with unusual grace for such a chubby kid.

"We got all summer to play," said Timmy, one of the guys I'd noticed earlier on the school playground.

"We got all summer," repeated Timmy's brother Tommy, nicknamed "Repeat."

I hadn't realized that they were two different guys when I had seen them at school. They looked exactly alike, with sandy-colored hair and blue eyes. They even sounded the same. The only way to tell them apart was that Repeat said everything his brother said. You knew that whoever spoke first must be Timmy.

All the guys had busted tools and were busily cleaning up the playground. As I moved in closer, though, I could see it wasn't a playground, not really. It was a baseball field. And it was a real mess.

Ham was cleaning the bleachers while Yeah-Yeah raked the infield. The twins cleared the outfield of trash, leaves, and twigs that had piled up over the long winter and wet spring.

This was a sandlot ballfield. *Their* ballfield.

"Hey, still in good shape, eh?" yelled Benny from across the sandlot. He was standing in left field, holding up a sign with big letters painted on it that said—"The Green Monster."

"Yeah-yeah, better shape than you," teased Yeah-Yeah, making the guys laugh again.

While they talked about baseball scores and who had first ups, I looked around the field.

A row of houses lined the far end. Every house had a fence. Probably to keep the ballplayers out, I guessed.

One backyard had the most awesome tree house I'd ever seen. It was built in the tallest tree around and looked down on practically the whole town. The tree house had walls, windows, and a cool ladder that could be pulled up to keep grown-ups out.

As I looked past the tree house at the neighboring yard, I began to shake. I was suddenly scared, and I didn't know why. That house and yard were hidden by a huge, faded green fence so high it cast big black shadows over the baseball field. But I couldn't see into the yard. I didn't want to, either.

I really got the creeps looking at that place.

"Finally, fifth grade is history, man!" cried Ham, startling me out of my trance.

"Ah! A hundred days of baseball," agreed Benny. "Think of

it guys, nothing but baseball morning, noon, and night. We got it made."

"We got all summer," said Timmy.

"We got all summer," said Repeat.

As the boys talked, they began a game of catch, tossing the ball around like experts. They moved slowly around the field, each finding his position. I could tell that they played a lot of ball here. It was like their home.

They never seemed to keep score... they didn't even have enough guys for two teams. It looked like one position was always left uncovered when someone was up. But somehow, it was still a game. It was like an endless dream game.

Every guy seemed to play well. But I could tell Benny was the best. No one had said so, but he seemed to be the leader of this baseball gang. And although I hardly knew these guys, I could already see why.

They didn't notice me standing by, so I decided to head back home.

Benny lived in the house across the street from me. Sitting on my front porch before dinner that night, I watched him heading down the street. Putting his hand on his front door, he turned and saw me watching. I wasn't sure, but I thought I saw him nod his head, just a little. Then he was gone. But it seemed as if he had noticed me.

That was a start.

I slammed my fist down hard, knocking the white marble off the shelf. I watched it roll, first slowly, then faster, down the desk and onto a tiny pulley. Up went one string, down came another. The marble was hoisted into the air, making a perfect landing into a tiny slingshot.

"Ready, aim, fire!" I cried, releasing the marble and sending it flying across the room.

"Ow! Hey, what the...?"

Uh-oh. Direct hit. Right into my mom's forehead. I never even saw her come in. It didn't hit her too hard, but I was sure in trouble now.

"Um, gee, sorry, Mom," I said, ducking my head a little.

"Scotty, I thought we talked about giving up this toy-machine stuff," Mom said, rubbing her forehead and dropping the marble into my hand. "You spend far too much time cooped up in your room, you know," she added.

"I know, Mom, I—"

"Honey," she interrupted, "have you made any friends yet?"

"No," I answered, not looking directly at her.

"Why not?"

"Well, I'm still the new guy in town... It's hard, Mom."

"You know, you won't make any friends sitting around here all summer, fiddling around with your catapults and motors. Like you did last summer. And the year before that."

The room was dark except for the light attached to my hard hat. Mom moved around the room, snapping on lights while she spoke.

She came back to where I sat and turned off my hat. She ruffled my hair. Moms love to do stuff like that.

"Scott, honey, you're a smart kid and I'm very proud of you. But you're a kid, don't forget, and kids need to get out and *play*."

"I—"

"Listen, I want to see you outdoors, getting fresh air, making friends. Heck, get into trouble once in a while like everyone else... well, not too much, but some, once in a while."

I peeked up at her. I was a little surprised.

"I bet you never heard of a mother giving her kid permission to get into trouble, huh?"

"Nope, I guess not."

"I want you to make friends this summer, okay pal?"

"But, Mom, I'm no good at making friends ... or anything. I mean, I'm just a lame old egghead—"

"And you'll always be a lame old egghead with an attitude like that. Promise you'll make some new friends?"

" 'Kay."

" 'Kay."

"Hey, Mom, do you think Bill—I mean Dad—might, you know, teach me to play ball?"

Mom's face lit up. My real dad died when I was little, and Bill was Mom's new husband. She had just gotten married the previous year, and that's why we moved to this new place. She wanted us to be a real family, but Bill and I were just getting used to each other. It might take a while.

"Are you kidding? He'd love to play ball with you. You know what an athlete he was in school."

Taking me by the hand and practically dragging me out of my room, Mom continued, "Why don't you go down and ask him right now?"

It was getting late, and the downstairs hallway was pitch black. Except for a speck of light at the end of the hall. It spilled out under the door to Bill's special room—his trophy room.

I gulped a couple of times, took a deep breath, and walked slowly up to the door. I knocked once, then twice. And waited.

"Come in," a voice boomed from behind the door.

"Hi, Dad...um, I mean Bill."

I never knew what to call the guy. Mom wanted me to call him Dad. But he was Bill to me. I didn't know him well yet. Didn't like him much, either. But to make Mom happy, I called him Dad—when she was around. When we were alone, he was Bill.

I stepped nervously into the room. This was the first time I had been in here. Bill was still unpacking. I was surprised to see ribbons, plaques, trophies—all kinds of neat stuff. The kind of stuff I figured someone cool would have—like maybe Benny.

"Um, I wondered if maybe, well, when you have some time, you could teach me how to play catch, like you said before?"

Not looking up from the trophy he was dusting, Bill grumbled, "Sure."

"Sure," I repeated in a whisper. "Okay, great. Um, thanks."

"Hmmm" came the reply.

There wasn't much else to do but leave. As I turned to go, I sneaked a peek back. Bill was dusting off an old-looking baseball and putting it on a fancy silver pedestal. Right there in the middle of all the other trophies.

I didn't care much about sports and wondered what all the fuss was over an old baseball. It even had a smudge on it. Why would Bill care about a dirty old baseball? As I walked back to my room, I figured I had a lot to learn about Bill.

● ● ●

The next morning, the alarm rang loudly in my ear. Even though it wasn't a school day, I raced out of bed, down the stairs, and out the front door. Looking up and down the quiet street, I noticed the chubby boy, Ham, buying a doughnut at a bakery truck down the block.

"Hey, wait up, guys! Come on!" he yelled, scrambling around the corner and out of sight.

I watched him jog down the street. I was ready to follow him when I looked down. Then I panicked. I still had my pajamas on! My cowboy ones, too! Man, what a nerd.

Racing back inside, I changed fast and then dug through my closet. Flinging toys and stuffed animals out of the way, I found what I was looking for. A baseball glove. A toy glove. It was all I had.

Next, I needed a baseball cap. I grabbed the closest thing I could find—my floppy fishing cap with the duck-billed visor and a big trout embroidered on the top.

I hurried back out to the street and ran through my new neighborhood. I slowed down for a minute as I passed the Little League field. Two teams were warming up on the field, dressed in neat uniforms. They looked like real baseball players. Not like the guys on the sandlot—Benny, Ham, and the gang. I picked up speed again and didn't stop until I came to the sandlot.

I found the secret opening easily this time and slid through quietly.

"Over here, throw it to me."

"You call that a throw?"

"My ups! My ups!"

The guys were playing baseball. As usual. I really wanted to play too, but they didn't know me. I didn't know them. I didn't even know how to play baseball!

I kind of stood there for a few minutes and just watched the action on the field. Benny was the best player, but they all seemed pretty good. To me, at least.

Slapping my hand into my mitt, I looked down at the

shrimpy little toy glove. What a stupid glove! What was I doing here, anyway?

As I wandered around the outside of the field, I watched the game. I didn't notice that I was standing next to a fence—a big green fence. *The* big green fence that had given me the creeps the day before.

I wasn't really looking where I was going, but suddenly I was afraid. I felt as though someone had punched me in the stomach, I was so scared. It was just like one of those horror movies, where the people know they shouldn't go upstairs, but *always* do. I didn't want to turn around, but I did. I was face-to-face, eye-to-eye with the fence.

There was a small hole right next to my eye, and I peered in. I was holding my breath. Little puffs of dirt and dust rose, but I couldn't really see what it was. A loud, weird sound was coming from inside—and it was getting closer.

There was something in there, something huge and angry and...hungry!

"Hey, look out!" came a cry in the distance.

Suddenly, I was back on the ballfield. I looked up, and the ball was flying through the blue sky. It was going really fast. And it was coming right at me!

I didn't know what to do. What could I do? It was headed straight for my head, and I wanted to run.

"You got it" came that same faraway voice.

"Yeah, send it back here when you get it, 'kay?" said another.

I couldn't believe it. They expected me—ME—to catch the ball!

That thing behind the fence scared me. But this terrified me. I couldn't move. I'd probably die, or go to the hospital or something.

At the very last second, I threw my arms over my face, my toy glove covering my head, and ducked. Not a very cool move.

The ball bounced off my glove, knocking me onto my butt,

hard. It landed, rolled, and stopped. At the fence. The big, green, scary fence.

"Nice catch," called Timmy, laughing hysterically.

"Nice catch," said Repeat, also laughing.

"Didya see that?" cried someone else, I didn't know who.

Everyone was laughing. This was definitely not how I'd planned to make new friends.

"Hey, kid! Let's go. Throw the ball back, willya?" Ham could hardly speak, he was laughing so hard.

"Yeah-yeah, hurry up."

"C'mon, throw it here."

"Let's go, let's go."

Shouts and laughter from the field got me back on my feet.

"'Kay, no sweat. I'll get it."

Ha! No sweat. I was practically drowning in my own sweat. But I had to be brave.

"Don't be a goofus—don't be a goofus—don't be a goofus," I whispered, moving toward the fence.

Before I reached out to grab the ball, I looked one more time through the tiny hole. I swore I could hear a monster breathing heavily, just waiting for me to become his lunch. Suddenly, something moved—and I didn't wait to see what it was!

I quickly grabbed the baseball and, like I'd seen these guys do, I tossed it. It stuck to my sweaty hand a little too long, flipped into the air, and landed near my own feet. Unfortunately, I didn't know how to throw, either.

I knew my chances of being on the team had disappeared with that throw. As they said in the schoolyard, I threw "like a girl!"

"My life is over," I whispered to myself as I turned to walk off the field, listening to hoots of laughter behind me.

Suddenly, the laughter stopped. Benny—the only guy who didn't laugh—was staring the guys down, making them feel bad for making fun of the new kid.

"Geez, Benny, you saw the way that kid threw the ball, didn't ya?" asked DeNunez.

DeNunez took off his glove as he spoke, flipping it over to Ham just the way I had done. This cracked the guys up all over again.

"Man, I swear, that kid's got the pantywaistiest arm I ever saw in my whole life," Ham, catching the glove, said seriously.

"I once seen a guy, threw like that," said Squints. "I mean, gaw, not that bad, but bad enough that he hadda move down to the fourth grade—everyone kept callin' him 'Bloomers'."

Benny looked sharply at the guys and, once again, they quieted down.

"I bet none of you bozos knows how Babe Ruth even got his nickname," said Benny.

"Aw that's easy. It's 'cause of the way he looked like a little kid 'n all," offered Ham.

"Naw, it's 'cause he held the bat real soft, just like a baby," suggested Timmy.

"Just like a baby," said Repeat.

"That's all bull. He just liked kids is all," came Bertram's answer.

"Uh, uh, wrong, no way," argued Squints. "The Babe was called The Babe because he was like the child of Yankee Stadium."

"You guys are so full of crap," said Benny, shaking his head. "I knew it. Let me tell you, George Herman Ruth got his nickname 'cause his mom died when he was a kid and he hadda go live in an orphanage."

The guys had never heard this story and they listened closely as Benny spoke.

"Nobody liked him there. He had no friends and no one stuck up for him. All the big guys picked on him. And when they messed with him, he couldn't fight back 'cause he was like, well, scared, y'know? Know what he'd do when they messed with him?"

Benny paused for a moment. Everyone leaned forward, waiting to hear what happened next.

"He cried. He cried when they beat him up, so they called him Babe."

The guys shook their heads slowly. Someone whistled. The Babe was their hero, the greatest baseball player that ever lived. But he was also a kid once—a wimpy kid, too. Or maybe, a kid just like them. They let it sink in as Benny continued.

"Now, how d'ya think that kid over there just felt, huh?"

I didn't know who this Babe Ruth was, but I sure wasn't about to ask. It seemed like a funny name to me. But these guys seemed to worship him. So I listened quietly to the story and silently thanked Benny for sticking up for me.

Benny was the first friend I made that summer—and the best friend, too. I figured, with Benny as my friend, I would become part of the team. I might really learn something about baseball. And maybe something about Babe Ruth, too.

The next morning I slurped my cereal quickly and loudly, thinking about baseball. "Dum de da da, ch-ch-ch," I hummed to myself, using my spoon and bowl as a drum set.

"Cut the racket, willya?" said Bill. "I'm trying to work."

I looked up and saw stacks of paperwork spread out in front of Bill. His forehead was puckered and he didn't look too happy, so I figured it must be important work.

Bill was on the road a lot with his job. I wasn't sure exactly what he did, but he must have been very good at it. Mom was always saying how proud she was of him. I'd heard him telling her about big sales meetings and regional offices. It all sounded very grown-up to me. I wasn't very interested.

"Sorry," I mumbled as I picked up my dishes and headed for the kitchen.

"So...?" asked my mom, raising her eyebrows. She looked at me as if we were sharing some kind of secret.

"Aw, he's too busy, Mom. He looks, well ..."

"Go on, honey, go back in and just ask. He'll take time out for you. Just ask him."

"Here we go again," I thought as I shuffled back through the swinging door. I didn't want to ask Bill to play catch. He looked too busy. But Mom wanted us to become friends.

"Um ... Bill?" I said, and I cleared my throat.

"Bill, could we, I mean, do you think you could, um ... like you said before, maybe...teach me to play, um, catch today?"

"Hmmm, yeah, sure. But later, okay? I gotta lot of work piling up that I gotta get done."

Well, it was a nice try.

"Okay, sure, thanks."

Just as I was about to get away, Mom came into the room, looking cheerful.

"Well, Bill, when are you going to teach our boy to play ball?"

"Mom, it's okay, he said..."

"Honey, I just told him I would, but later. I've got a big deadline with this work, and I'm really under the gun, ya know?"

"Nonsense. How long could it take? You can't spare a half hour..."

"Mom, really ..."

"...to toss the ball around, to show him a little something?"

Bill rolled his eyes and dropped his pen.

This was not going to be fun. I had just been "Mom-embarrassed" and there was no way out of it. Why couldn't she leave things alone? She was clueless. In fact, she actually thought she had helped me! Boy, I sure didn't need that kind of help.

"Sure, fine. C'mon, I'll get my glove."

"See? All settled, boys," said Mom. To me, she winked and whispered, "Told you so."

Outside in the backyard, Bill easily slid his hand into his glove, popping the ball in and out like a real pro. I had a bad feeling about this.

"Keep your eye on the ball. Okay, put the glove up...no, up higher where the ball is gonna go."

"Okay, yeah, I think I've got it. Shoot."

Bill threw the ball. I swung my glove to the right. The ball went to the left. I missed by a mile.

"Sorry, Bill." I knew I was no good at this.

"Okay, all right, that's okay. Just throw it back and we'll try again." Bill looked at his watch, and I knew he was wondering when he could get back to his real work.

After the lousy throw I had made to the guys, I decided to walk the ball back to Bill. He was surprised, but didn't say anything. I was glad.

"Okay, I'm ready again."

"Um, yeah. Keep your eye on the ball and put the glove where the ball goes, Scott." Bill again tossed the ball to me softly.

"Darn, my glove…" The ball had landed on the webbing, tearing the skimpy little glove in two.

"Hey, not bad, not bad. At least you followed the ball. Now throw it back this time."

I tossed the ball back. It was a lame throw. Just like yesterday. It rolled to Bill's feet.

"Oh, brother," said Bill. He couldn't believe how bad I was.

The next throw was harder, faster than the first two. And was heading right for me. I wanted to yell or scream. But I didn't even have time for that.

I put my hand up, but the torn toy glove was not much help. The ball was coming fast.

"Aggghhh!" The ball hit my eye with a loud thud.

That was the end of our game.

As I staggered toward the house, I thought I heard Benny from behind the fence. He said something like "Aw! What a jerk!" Somehow, I didn't think he was talking about me… was he talking about Bill? Had he been watching?

After calming Mom down, we stuck a huge steak on my eye for an hour. Mom always said that a cold piece of meat was better than ice to bring the swelling down. She was right. I started feeling pretty good about my new black eye. After all, it was a real sports injury.

Then I remembered the lousy attempt at a catch I'd made, and I felt crummy all over again.

"Smalls, we're gonna play some ball. We need an extra guy. You game?"

I looked up and there was Benny, standing at the porch steps.

"Um, naw, thanks anyway."

"Why not? Doncha like baseball?"

"Well, yeah, sure, but ..."

"But nothing. C'mon."

I wanted to go. But I was scared. I had already made a fool of myself with the guys. I didn't think baseball was my game.

"But my glove, it's busted, ya know. So, thanks, but I can't go."

Benny pulled something from his back pocket and smiled at me.

"Here ya go," Benny said, handing me a glove. A *real* glove, too.

"But..." I started to say.

"S'okay, take it. I got a extra one."

I was going to play baseball! Yelling through the screen door, I told my mom that I was going to the sandlot and Benny and I took off, running down the street. It was my first real ballgame.

We stopped at the store to buy a new ball and a pack of Bazooka gum. Then we caught up with the gang. They were all chewing loudly on huge wads of gum. They had so much gum in their mouths, they could barely talk.

Ham, the joker, chewed on a candy cigar.

"Check it out, boys, I'm the Great Bambino."

Everyone laughed as he strutted around, his fat belly sticking out and the cigar dangling from his teeth.

"Who's that?" I asked, wanting to be part of this fun.

The laughter suddenly stopped. Eight guys turned to stare at me. I wasn't sure what I had done, but I thought it had to do with this Great Bambino guy.

"What?" Ham began, looking around the group. "What did he say?"

"Where'd you come from anyway, kid, a cave?" asked

Bertram squinting at me through his thick, Coke-bottle glasses.

"Yeah-yeah, you from Mars or somethin'?"

"Ain't you never heard of the Sultan of Swat?"

"The Titan of Terror?"

"The Colossus of Clout!"

"The Colossus of Clout!"

All around me, nicknames were being spit out like chewing gum. These guys couldn't believe I could be so lame—so stupid.

Even Benny was shocked.

"The King of Krash?" he asked, eyes widening in surprise.

I had no idea who they were talking about.

"Oh, the Great Bambino," I lied. I had to think fast or these guys would know how stupid I was. "Sure, of course, I thought you said the Great Bambi!"

"Eww! That wimpy deer?" Ham pinched his nose and made a face.

"Yeah, well, I guess. Sorry."

Looking around the group, I felt like a total jerk. These guys were cool. They chomped their chewing gum and spat on the ground like they were chewing tobacco. I tried to spit like them, but all that came out was a little trickle running down my chin.

"Scotty, this here's Squints, Ham, Kenny, Yeah-Yeah, Bertram, Timmy, and his brother Tommy. We call him Repeat. Guys, this is Scotty Smalls." Benny introduced me around.

"He makes nine. Now we got a real team," Benny added. I was glad he was on my side. I was still not sure about the other guys, though. They didn't seem to like me much.

We walked to the sandlot, with me tagging along behind everyone. But I could hear everything they said.

"Whatd'ya bring him along for, Benny?" asked Bertram.

"Hey, I told you. We had eight, now he makes nine."

"So would my grandmother but I ain't bringing her."

"Nine guys, we got a whole team," Benny insisted.

"Naw. With Georgie Elswenger we had a whole team—and at least he could throw," Ham chimed in.

"He ain't no good, Benny. The kid can't throw for nothin'," said DeNunez, glancing over his shoulder at me. I looked away.

"Benny, you're our extra guy," Timmy added. "I mean, you already covered Georgie's spot ever since Elswenger moved to Arizona."

"So, now I rotate eight positions instead of seven. I could always use the practice."

"No way, man. It's stupid. This kid is a major weenie," said Squints as they reached the field.

"Right, Squints, and you're Willie freaking Mays! Y'know, you catch like a dork—anybody ever bust your chops 'bout that?"

"No, but, well, you know... I mean I'm..." Squints trailed off, looking around for help.

"And you, Yeah-Yeah, you run like a duck..."

"'Kay, I know, but I'm..."

"Part of the team."

All I wanted was to be part of the team and, somehow, Benny knew this. He made the guys understand it, too.

I ran out to left field. We began to play baseball.

The ball began to fly around the bases, thrown from one guy to the next. It went fast. But the team was even faster. They always caught the ball. No one ever dropped it.

Except me, of course. I stood in left field, waiting for my turn. Benny would bat the ball toward me. I wanted to catch it, to prove that I could do it. But every time the ball came toward me, I ducked. I was afraid. And I still had a black eye from playing catch with Bill.

I couldn't throw the ball, either. Whenever it came my way, I would pick it up and carry it back in. I handed it to the nearest player and ran back out to my position. The guys were getting kind of mad by now, but I simply didn't know how to throw. I tugged at my fishing cap and watched the ball go around the bases.

"Smalls, man, what gives?" asked Benny as he trotted out to the field where I stood. "You *can* throw the ball, ya know!"

"Um, no, I can't," I admitted, feeling as though I would cry. "I don't know how. Thanks anyway, though, it was fun...."

I turned to walk away. I thought he would kick me off the team. But he didn't.

"Wait a minute, kid," Benny said, grabbing my arm. "You think too much. I bet you even get straight A's and stuff, am I right?"

"No... I got a B one time. Well, it was really an A minus, but it shoulda been a B," I answered.

"Well, stop thinkin' and start playin'. Throw the ball like you'd throw a newspaper.... You ever have a paper route?"

"I helped..."

"Okay, throw the ball like it was a crumpled-up paper," he said.

"But how do I catch it?" I asked.

"Don't worry. Just stand there and stick your glove in the air. I'll take care of the rest!" he said as he ran back to the infield.

Benny's advice worked. I still didn't throw very hard, but I was able to get the ball back to my teammates. And when Benny hit the ball toward me, I stood still and kept my glove up. Wow! I caught it the first time!

I now felt as if I was a part of the team. We played ball nonstop, every day. Benny taught me how to stand when I was at bat. He taught me how to swing. I even learned to hit the ball!

I worked on everything Benny showed me. I really practiced. After one month of playing every day, I saw that I wasn't just some dumb nerd. I could actually play ball.

I still didn't know who the Great Bambino was. But I figured if I just listened and hung around the guys, I would learn all there was to know about baseball.

CHAPTER

4

I stood at my usual place in left field. We had a hot game going in the sandlot. Ham was at bat. Kenny was pitching. I had been playing with the guys for weeks now and was starting to get better. They would actually throw the ball to me. Kenny was throwing great that day, and he was about to strike Ham out.

Ham waited for the next pitch. He swung. *CRACK!* He hit the ball. It was flying out toward me. I kept my eyes on it and tried to get underneath to catch it. But it was too fast and too high. It looked like it was going to be a home run!

The ball dropped over the fence behind me. It was the scary green fence. I had been running toward it when I stopped short. I gulped and felt nervous. But I knew it was our only ball. I didn't want the game to end. So I walked over to the fence, sweating and scared, and started to climb.

"NOOOO!" came a loud scream from behind.

"Stop!" shouted someone else.

Eight pairs of arms reached out and pulled me away from the green fence. What did I do now?

"Holy schmoley, you coulda been killed!" said Squints.

"Yeah-yeah—truly!" agreed Yeah-Yeah.

"Whaddya think you're doin', anyway?" asked Ham.

"Well, you know, the ball ... " I started to answer.

"You gotta be kiddin'!" said Squints.

"Y'know, you can't go over that fence, Smalls," said Benny.

"So how d'we get the ball back?" I asked.

"We don't," said Timmy.

"We don't," repeated Repeat.

"It's outta here," said Timmy.

"It's outta here," said Repeat.

"Kiss it good-bye," said Timmy.

"Kiss it—" started Repeat.

"Aw, shut up, Tommy!" said Timmy.

"Yeah, that ball is history," said Bertram.

"Forever," said Ham. "Just forget it."

"Okay guys, game's over. We'll get a new ball tomorrow," said Benny.

I stood there, surprised. These guys played baseball all day every day. But now they were ready to go home. Even Benny. Just because the ball went over the fence. I couldn't believe it.

"Why?" I asked.

"THE BEAST," they all said at the same time. I felt a shiver of fear run up my back.

But I had to know what they were talking about. Slowly, I walked back to the fence. I put my eye right up against the hole and looked in. There were hundreds of little craters in the soft dirt. The craters had been made by baseballs. But they were all empty. I could see our ball lying on the ground.

Out of nowhere came a huge, hairy paw. It didn't look like any ordinary dog or cat paw. It must be the Beast!

The paw grabbed the ball. It was gone. The only thing left was a crater. Just like all the others.

"Whoaaa! What was that?" I screamed. I ran back to the guys.

They looked at one another for a moment and, all at the same time, said, "Campout."

I had never been on a campout before, but the big tree house I had noticed on the day school let out belonged to the twins. This was where the gang would sleep out or have important meetings. After dinner that night, we all met there to have an important meeting.

"You want s'more?" asked Ham as I sat down next to him.

"Some more of what?" I asked right back. I hadn't had anything yet—how could I have more?

"Man, you kill me," Ham laughed. "Kid doesn't even know what a s'more is! Here, look, these are s'mores."

He pointed to a goopy mess of graham crackers, marshmallow, and chocolate. He heated it up on a stick over a Boy Scout camping stove. Then he popped it into his mouth. It was so messy, most of it dripped down his chin. But he licked his lips and patted his belly.

"Mmmm," he said, already making another s'more.

I looked around the tree house. It was really cool. It looked as if they had a lot of meetings up here. Posters and photos were stuck all over the walls. They were mostly of famous baseball players, but there were a few girls in bikinis, too. An old table and some wobbly chairs were set up in the corner. But we all just sat around on the floor, on our sleeping bags.

"Yeah, all right, guys. Listen up," said Squints, turning the camping lantern down low.

"I'm gonna tell you a story, Smalls. First time DeNunez heard it he barfed," Squints said.

"Did not," DeNunez said.

"Did too, man," said Benny.

Everyone shut up, waiting for Squints to start again.

"When Yeah-Yeah heard it he peed his pants," Squints said.

"Wait a minute, I..." Yeah-Yeah said.

"You did, Yeah-Yeah, but that's not the point. Point is, I'm gonna tell you the scariest story you ever heard. I'm gonna tell you the legend of the Beast," said Squints.

He was right. It was the scariest story I had ever heard. I sat very still. With the lantern turned low and the wind blowing outside the tree house, I could almost see the Beast. I hung onto every word.

Squints told a story that had begun many years before. It happened in a place called Mertle's Acres, a big junkyard filled with rusty old cars and broken refrigerators. But there were lots of cool things there too, like fighter-plane parts, cargo ships, and motorcycles. The stuff in Mertle's Acres was worth a fortune. At least it was to Mertle.

Mertle had to protect his junkyard. So he bought a dog. It wasn't just any old dog. He was a mean dog. Even as a puppy, he was bad. Always getting in fights. Squints said he even killed three dogs by the time he was only four months old.

Mertle knew this dog was for him. He needed to keep thieves out of his junkyard so they wouldn't steal. With a big, ugly dog like this one, he knew he was safe.

The dog—or the Beast, as we always called him—was huge! Mertle would feed him garbage bags full of raw meat to keep him growing. But Mertle wanted him to stay mean, too. So he left him all alone. He was never, ever allowed to go out of the junkyard. And Mertle never went to visit or play with him, only to drop off food. Nobody liked the Beast. And the Beast didn't like anybody, either.

One night, two robbers sneaked into the junkyard. They were quiet, but the Beast heard them anyway. Before they could even scream, the Beast jumped, showing his teeth and growling. He dragged them into the darkness.

No one ever saw the robbers again.

This happened a lot. People were always trying to steal from Mertle's Acres. But the Beast was always there to stop them.

Soon, the police went to see Mertle. So far, there were thirty-seven people missing and the cops figured the Beast had something to do with it. They searched Mertle's Acres. But they never found a single person.

The Beast had eaten them. Bones and all!

Even though the Beast was only doing his job of keeping people out, he wasn't supposed to eat them. So the police said he couldn't do it anymore.

Mertle had to take him out of the junkyard and lock him

up in his own backyard. The Beast could never come out again. He had to stay chained up forever.

"And so, the Beast sits there in the backyard—right next door!" said Squints, finishing the story. "He dreams of the day he can break his chains and chase down kids—and kill again!"

The whole gang was quiet. Some had their eyes shut. Others were shaking. I checked my pants to be sure I hadn't peed them.

"See, that's why you can't ever go there. Nobody has and nobody will," said Bertram.

"Naw, one kid tried," said Ham. "Nobody ever seen him again, though."

"Bull—" said DeNunez.

"I swear," said Ham. "He got eaten!"

"Yeah-yeah," said Yeah-Yeah. "That was the kid who went to get his kite, right?"

"Name was Boogers Fleming," said DeNunez.

"Naw, man, it was the guy had all the warts on his face," said Timmy.

"Davy the Toad," said Repeat.

"That's what I said," said Timmy.

"Yeah, poor old Toad," said Squint.

"Never saw him again," added Bertram.

I felt a little sick to my stomach. But I didn't want to barf. Not in front of the guys.

"Nuh-uh," I said. "That ain't true. You guys are trying to scare me, and I—"

"Oh, yeah?" demanded Squints. "C'mere. Stick your head over the side there and just look."

I leaned out the tree-house window. It was too late to back out now. Besides, I wanted to see what the Beast looked like. So I looked.

There, in the other yard, was a huge chain. A gigantic bathtub full of water was next to it. I could see dust puffing up and down, but I didn't wait to see where it came from. I had seen enough.

"He's down there!" I screamed. Then, taking a deep breath, I tried to be calm. "He's down there," I repeated, more quietly this time.

"Yup, just like I told you," said Squints.

"Whatever goes over that fence stays there," said Ham. "And we don't go after it."

"It belongs to the Beast...forever!" added Squints.

I knew it must be true. The guys claimed that more than 150 baseballs had gone over that fence. And I couldn't see one of them when I looked out of the tree house that night. It had to be the Beast.

We needed a new ball. The sandlot was a great place to play, but we were always losing balls over Old Man Mertle's fence. We couldn't get them back, so each guy took a turn getting a new one.

It was Yeah-Yeah's turn this time.

"What took you guys so long?" asked Benny. He was always the first one on the field. He couldn't wait to play.

"Squints was droolin' over a girl!" said Yeah-Yeah.

"Shut up! I was not," argued Squints.

"Oh, yeah? Then why'd you practically faint when Wendy Peffercorn walked by, huh?" Yeah-Yeah continued. "Your tongue was scrapin' the sidewalk!"

Squints had a big crush on an "older woman." Wendy Peffercorn was nineteen and beautiful. We all had it bad for her. And Squints had it the worst. But he would never admit it.

"Oh, Wendy, my sweetheart, my darling..." Yeah-Yeah teased Squints. The whole gang was laughing and poking Squints.

Squints tried to tackle Yeah-Yeah, but Ham grabbed his shoulders.

"Hold me back, man! Hold me back," Squints yelled.

"I *am* holdin' you back, Squints," said Ham.

"Oh... well, let me go, then," said Squints.

"So where'd you come up with the money for the ball, Yeah-Yeah?" asked DeNunez, changing the subject.

"Yeah-yeah! It was so great! I, like, went around to houses, you know, pretending I was selling magazine—what do you call those things—prescriptions, subscriptions—for school," Yeah-Yeah explained.

"People asked if they should pay me now, and I said yeah-yeah, pay me now!" he continued. "So they did!"

"No way!" said Ham.

"Get outta here! How could ya do that?" said Bertram.

"Yeah-yeah, I know. I'll take the money back. It was kind of crummy to do, but I had no money and…" explained Yeah-Yeah.

"Aw, forget it, man," said Benny. "These guys are just mad they didn't think of it first."

"Yeah, you know how many lawns I hadda mow when I had to buy the ball? Geez," said Ham.

It was a very hot day. So hot that we only played a couple of innings before everyone was sweating. We were soaking wet from running around in the hot sun. It was not a good day to play ball.

"I can't take it no more, Benny," wailed Ham. "I'm fryin' like an egg!"

"C'mon, boys, don't be a bunch of wimps!" said Benny.

Benny would play in any weather. He'd play in the middle of the winter if he could.

"Benny, face it," said Squints. "We can't play no more; we'll all melt. It's time to call it a day."

"Let's vote, then," said Benny. "Anyone that wants to be a baby-faced, pantywaist, wear-your-mamma's-girdle, raise your hand."

We all raised our hands.

It was settled. We raced to the *only* place to be on such a hot day—the pool. It was a good way to cool off. And, even better, it was where all the girls hung out.

KERSPLASH!

Ham leaped off the edge of the pool, holding his knees.

"Hamonball!" he screamed as he hit the water.

He created such a huge splash that all the girls lying around the poolside got soaked. They screamed at Ham. He pretended not to notice. He was having too much fun.

The water felt great. We played chicken fights and sub attack. We swam and jumped and splashed. It was a perfect summer day, and we made the most of it.

But the water wasn't the *real* reason the gang went to the pool. It was the lifeguard.

Wendy Peffercorn. The girl of Squints'—and all the guys'—dreams.

"Oh, man," said Benny.

"Yeah-yeah, look at her puttin' suntan lotion on!" said Yeah-Yeah.

"She don't know what she's doin'," said Timmy.

"She don't know what she's doin'," said Repeat.

"Oh, yeah she does," said Benny. "She knows what she's doin' and she knows what we're thinkin'."

Sloshing around the pool was just an excuse to look at her. She sat high up in the lifeguard chair. She wore dark sunglasses and her blond hair was pulled back in a ponytail. She was incredible. I had never seen a girl like this before. I could see why the guys liked to come to the pool.

But Squints was the one who really had the hots for Wendy.

"I can't take this no more!" Squints suddenly yelled.

He pulled himself out of the pool and walked quickly to the diving board. He stuck his chest out as he passed Wendy.

"Whatsa matter with him?" I asked the guys.

"What's he think he's doin'?" asked Ham.

"Don't know," answered Yeah-Yeah. "But that board is at the deep end. And Squints don't know how to swim too good!"

We watched Squints climb the board and walk to the end. It was as if he were walking the plank in a pirate movie. The pool was a great place to play on a hot day, but none of the guys were very good swimmers. And no one had *ever* gone off the deep end.

Squints looked around. He should have been scared. But when he looked at Wendy in the lifeguard chair, he got a stupid grin on his face. What was he doing? What could we do?

I noticed Wendy smiling back at Squints. Then, grabbing his nose, Squints leaped off the board. He sailed through the air for a moment. Then he landed. Hard. He hit the water and went under…and under…and under. He didn't come up. He just sank like a stone!

"Squints!" screamed Bertram.

"Holy cow! He's drowning!" yelled Ham.

We jumped out of the water and ran over to the deep end. We were waving our arms and screaming. Everyone around the pool looked up and followed us to where Squints used to be.

Wendy the lifeguard jumped out of her chair and into the water in one smooth move. She went under and came up empty-handed. On her second try, she surfaced with Squints, lying still in her arms.

After pulling him out of the water, Wendy started to give Squints mouth-to-mouth resuscitation. This looked serious.

We stood by watching. We were afraid that it was too late for Squints.

Then, as we waited, Squints peeked up at us. He winked! What was he up to now?

While Wendy was bent down in her effort to save Squints' life, he grabbed her and gave her a huge, sloppy kiss. Right on the lips!

Everyone around gasped. Then laughed. Squints had been faking it all along.

"You little pervert!" said Wendy.

She grabbed him by the neck and carried him over to the exit.

"Get outta here, kid," she yelled. "And your friends, too. And don't ever come back, either!"

We ran out of the pool, laughing and slapping one another's backs. Even though Squints had done a rotten thing by pretending he had drowned, we respected him. It was cool. And it was the closest he or any of us would ever get to Wendy Peffercorn.

That night, we all crowded into the Boys' Club along with a hundred other guys to see the movie *King Kong*. In the dark, cramped room it was hard to see very much. Beat-up old chairs were shoved up next to each other. We sat shoulder to shoulder, breathing heavily from the heat. Other than the chairs, a big white sheet that served as the movie screen, and an old, frayed banner, the Boys' Club was bare. I squinted through the dark at the banner, which hung in the far corner. The letters were so faded that they were mostly gone, and all I could read was " O S' LU ."

The gang never had much use for the club. Once in a while they would show a good movie, but why waste time indoors when there was a perfectly good baseball field to play on?

This was the first time any of us had seen *King Kong*. Our eyes widened with fear as the huge ape tramped through the jungle. As we sat there, each one of us secretly thought of Mertle's Beast. It made the movie even scarier.

"Eee! Eee! Ooo! Ooo! Ooo!" shouted Ham as we left the Boys' Club. "I'm King Kong," he said as he jumped up and down.

We pounded him with our fists, pretending to fight off the famous ape.

"Hey, cool it, guys," he said as he ducked. "I'm only kidding. Do I look like a monkey to you?"

"Yeah, and ya smell like one, too," said someone behind Ham.

"Hey. Look, guys, if it ain't the sandlot babies!" said another voice. We turned around.

A group of guys had wandered over while we were horsing

around. We could tell they were Little Leaguers because of their matching caps and shirts.

My gang didn't play in Little League. They had tried out before and were good enough to make the league. In fact, they all made it, no sweat. But when they found out they'd be playing on different teams, they quit. The guys wanted to play together. They would only play together. So they played at the sandlot.

"Shut up, blockheads," said Ham.

"Whatcha gonna do, porker, sit on me?" said the first Little Leaguer.

"Hey, Rodriguez, man, why you still hanging with these dorks?" the second Little Leaguer asked Benny. "You could be playing with us. Real official—real baseball," he continued.

"Yeah, Benny," said the first one. "You'd make the All-Star team easy. It's the big time!"

"Play us and you'll see, Phillips," answered Benny.

"You gotta be kiddin'!" said the first one. "Forget it. We only play with real ballplayers—not guys with a bunch of toy bats and Wiffle balls!"

Laughing, the Little Leaguers walked away. We stood silently for a minute.

"Hey, Benny," asked Squints. "We gonna let them get away with that?"

"For now," Benny answered. "For now. Let's go."

"So, you guys think he really died at the end?" I asked as we started walking home. I was still thinking about the movie.

"Who?" asked Benny.

"King Kong," I answered.

"No way," said Squints. "He's too big. To him, fallin' off the Empire State's just like fallin' off a roof."

"Yeah, he's alive," agreed Ham.

"So... where d'ya think he is now?" I asked.

"Mmm, probably back in the jungle," said Bertram, scratching his head.

"Sure, probably," said Timmy.

"Probably," said Repeat.

I thought for a moment, then said, "Hey, has anyone ever really *seen* the Beast?"

I didn't notice that everyone had stopped. I walked a few steps, realized I was alone, and turned around.

"What?" I asked.

"Look, Smalls," explained Squints. "You don't gotta see something to know it's real, y'know? I mean, King Kong is real, right?"

"Yeah, sure..." I answered.

"So nobody has to see the Beast to know he's real."

"You don't think the Beast is..." I hesitated. "King Kong?"

No one had ever thought of that before. Could it be? We never really saw the Beast. And King Kong was out there somewhere.

Looking around at each other, we suddenly noticed where we were. Right in front of Mertle's!

"No way," said Squints.

"Gaw, what a dumb idea!" agreed Ham.

"Man, I almost felt like a dufes there for a minute," said Bertram.

We quickly headed home, agreeing that it was a crazy idea. And we were relieved. But my heart was still pounding when I went to bed that night.

Sitting in Benny's living room the next day, with the TV blasting, we were worried only about baseball.

Benny's hero Maury Wills was on first base, ready to steal second. We leaned forward, all eyes on the TV screen, waiting to see this great move.

"Yeah-yeah, he's gonna go, he's gonna go!" said Yeah-Yeah.

"Not yet, he ain't," said Benny, never looking away from the TV.

"Now, now, just watch, he's gonna do it, he's gonna go!" the guys were screaming now, waiting for Wills to steal another base and set a new record.

"Not yet," said Benny again.

He stared at Wills on TV, squinting his eyes. He leaned forward a little. He kept watching.

"Okay, he's gonna go... riiiiight... nooooowww!" he yelled as Wills left first base and raced to second. Wills made it. He'd set another record.

We all just looked at Benny as if he had stolen the base himself.

"How'd ya do that?" I asked.

"How did you know when he'd go, man?" asked Squints.

All the guys wanted to know what Benny's trick was.

But Benny just smiled. He just knew a lot about baseball. More than we ever would, probably.

CHAPTER
6

The sound of squeaky wheels surprised us.

As usual, we were all at the sandlot, in our regular positions. We'd just started the first game of the day when a bunch of Little Leaguers pulled up on their bikes.

They watched us silently. Benny was in a pickle. He loved getting into a pickle because he was the best at getting out. Ham was playing third, and Repeat was catching. Benny weaved back and forth, moved right, then left. He rubba-legged. Ham and Repeat had no chance. With the ball still in Ham's mitt, Benny crossed home easily. The rest of the guys might be good ballplayers, but Benny was in a league of his own.

"It's easy to look good when ya only play with babies and fat boys...or yourselves," yelled one of the Little Leaguers. I recognized him from the *King Kong* movie at the Boys' Club.

"Whatcha say, jerk?" Benny asked, walking right up to the guy.

"He said they're garbage. They shouldn't even be allowed to *touch* a baseball," said another Little Leaguer.

We were all mad, but Ham couldn't stand it anymore.

"Come on! Right here, right now," he yelled, running over with his fists held up. "Come on, boys, are ya chicken?"

"Ha!" said the first Little Leaguer. "We play real baseball, on a real baseball diamond. You losers ain't even good enough to carry our bats."

"Watch yer mouth, jerk," said Benny.

"Shut up, creepface," said a Little Leaguer.

"Weenie!" yelled Benny.

"Stinkweed!"

"Snotface!"

"Dog-doo-for-breakfast-eating loser!"

"You mix your Wheaties with spit!"

"You bob for apples in your toilet—and you like it!"

We looked from Benny to the Little League guy as they passed insults back and forth. That last one was a doozy. We waited. It was Benny's turn.

"YOU PLAY BALL LIKE A GIRL!"

Nobody spoke. That was the ultimate baseball insult. No ballplayer would take that lying down.

The Little Leaguer put his face right into Benny's.

"What did you say?" he whispered.

"You heard me," Benny replied coolly.

"Tomorrow. Sunup. At *our* ballfield. Not your stinkin' little sandlot. Be there, buffalo-butt breath," said the Little Leaguer.

"Count on it, you pee-drinking dorkface," shouted Benny. The Little League guys were already riding away.

Benny kicked the ground and looked up at us. He was grinning from ear to ear.

"Looks like we got us a ballgame, boys."

We threw our caps in the air and cheered.

The grass on the Little League Field was still wet from the dew when we arrived at dawn the next morning.

"PLAY BALL," Ham shouted. The game began.

The Little Leaguers were up first. DeNunez was pitching. He struck out the first batter.

"Whiffer, whiffer, whiffer," the guys chanted in the outfield. We were trying to psych the next batter into striking out.

It didn't work. He hit the ball, sending a grounder to Yeah-Yeah at shortstop.

Yeah-Yeah picked up the ball and fired it to first base. Timmy caught it easily. Batter two was out.

DeNunez pitched to batter number three. He swung and hit a slow fly to the outfield.

"I got it, I got it," Bertram and I said at the same time.

We weren't watching where we were going. We were too busy tracking the ball. We were running right at each other. Luckily, before we crashed into each other, we stopped. But the ball dropped. Right between us.

"What ya doin', man?" said Bertram.

"I thought you said you got it," I said.

"Somebody better get it," Benny yelled to us. The batter had passed second and was on his way to third base.

I scooped the ball into my mitt and fired it with all the strength I had. I guess all those zillions of games we'd played this summer were finally paying off.

The ball flew into home. It slammed into Ham's mitt a second before the batter slid over the plate.

"Yer out!" yelled Ham. "Yer dead! Gone! Kaput! To the moon! Over and out!"

He strutted around, sticking his thumb in the batter's face. Ham always got a little overly excited when he made a good play. He shut up quickly when he noticed everyone staring at him, though. Enough was enough.

"Um, you're out," he said calmly. We were up next.

Benny was first at bat. He really showed those clowns how to play baseball. He belted the first pitch straight out of the park.

"That's one, fellas," he called as he ran the bases. "Get used to it."

The Little Leaguers could never get used to it. We pumped one ball after another. We made run after run. We were awesome. We were a team. And we beat the heck out of those boys. The final score was 12 to 4. I even got two hits and caught a couple of flies. It felt good.

● ● ●

To celebrate our baseball superiority, we went to the town carnival that night.

"Bang, zoom, outta here!" Benny said as we walked around the dazzling midway, checking out the rides.

"You see the looks on their faces? Didya? Man, it was like, 'duh, so *that's* how you play baseball ...'"

"Heh, heh, they really are *Little* Leaguers now," agreed Squints.

"Whoa, I almost forgot the chaw, boys!" said Bertram. He took a package out of his pocket and passed it around.

It was chewing tobacco. Not bubble gum, like they usually chewed. It was the real thing. The kind the pros chewed when they played. We were celebrating.

"I been saving it for a good time," said Bertram.

"What is it?" I asked. There was still a lot about the game of baseball I didn't know.

"Geez, Smalls, what gives?" said Ham. "Next you're gonna tell us you don't know who the Babe is, either."

Actually, I still hadn't figured out this Babe Ruth character. Of course, I didn't admit it.

Everyone took a pinch of the stuff as Bertram passed it around.

"What d'ya do with it?" I asked. I was really confused.

"You're killin' me, kid," Ham laughed. "You chew it, of course!"

"All the pros do it," added DeNunez.

"Yeah-yeah, gives ya lots of energy," said Yeah-Yeah.

"Smooth," said Benny. His cheeks were stuffed with the chaw.

"Mmm, juicy," agreed Ham.

"Tangy," said Squints.

"Tastes kinda like an ashtray smells," I said. I couldn't see what all the fuss was about.

"S'posed to," said DeNunez. He seemed to be the expert.

We walked and chewed our tobacco. We were the best ball-team in town, and we had proved it today.

A loud buzz and flashing lights grabbed our attention.

"Let's ride!" we all said together.

The Tilt-a-Whirl was the fastest, coolest ride at the carnival. Naturally, that was the ride we'd go on.

And boy, we went. So did our breakfast, lunch, and dinner. It spewed all over the place. The combination of chewing tobacco and Tilt-a-Whirl was deadly. One by one, we all barfed as the ride kept spinning. Screams could be heard all over the carnival as people were hit with sudden glops of vomit. It was not a pretty sight. It would be a long time before anyone mentioned chaw again.

Moaning and sweating, I wobbled down the stairs the next morning. Mom and Bill were at the front door.

"Okay, I'll be back in a half hour, honey," Mom said. "I'm taking Dad to the airport."

"Hmmm, 'kay," I said. I still felt lousy. "Where you goin'?"

"Chicago, on business," answered Bill. "I'll be gone for a week. Listen, Scott, while I'm gone, you're the man of the house. Understand?"

"Yeah, sure, Bill—er Da—um, okay, I guess so." With Mom and Bill both there, I had no idea what to call him. But he had put me in charge. I was feeling a little better.

"We'll take another crack at catch when I get back, okay, sport?" he said. "Take care of things while I'm gone. I'm counting on you."

He shook my hand.

Heading over to the sandlot later, we stopped by the store for bubble gum, the kind that had eight baseball cards in each pack. Gum was about the only thing we'd be chewing anymore.

"Who'd you get?" asked Squints as we opened our packs.

"A Mickey Mantle and seven guys I ain't never heard of," said Ham.

"I got a Brooks Robinson and a Koufax. Not bad," Squints said.

"Aw, mine's all junk," said Bertram.

"Same here," added DeNunez. "I got some duds, too."

"Yeah-yeah, one Whitey Ford 'n seven bombs," said Yeah-Yeah.

"Hey, Ben—" Squints started to ask.

But Benny's face had turned white. He just stood there, staring at his baseball cards. His mouth was wide open. Shuffling the cards one by one, over and over, Benny looked up slowly.

"You okay, man?" Squints asked.

Benny handed Squints the cards. Squints looked at the baseball cards once, then twice. He whistled and handed the cards around for the rest of us to see.

"Oh, my gaw…" Squints began. He whistled again.

"Sonofagun!" said Ham.

"Unfrigginbelievable!" said Timmy.

"Unfrigginbelievable!" said Repeat. "Don't tell Ma I said that, okay?"

"I won't," said Timmy.

Almost every single card in Benny's pack was the same. He had gotten five Maury Wills cards. His hero! His idol! And he had five of him in one pack.

It was a miracle. We all knew it. We didn't know what it meant, but we figured it must have meant something.

Squints, who never went anywhere without his radio tuned in to a ballgame, pulled the plug out of his ear and hollered.

"Oh geez … oh geez! This is unreal! Maury Wills just stole his seventy-fifth base!"

"Let's play ball!" yelled Benny. "I gotta play. NOW!"

We arrived at the sandlot and hurried out to our positions. Benny picked up the bat and got ready for his pitch. DeNunez wound up and threw the ball. Hard and fast.

Benny swung. And then the miracle happened.

The ball exploded. It didn't just rip or tear. Benny had burst the baseball with one swing. It flew through the infield, swirling and falling to pieces as it went.

"Awesome!" said Bertram. We all just stared at Benny like he was a hero.

"Naw, it ain't," said Benny.

"Sure is, Ben," said Squints. "Hardly anybody, anytime ever busted the guts outta a ball. It's a miracle. That's what the Wills cards meant."

"Alls it means is we don't have a ball. We can't play no more. I just blew the whole day for us," Benny said as he threw the bat to the ground. He hated to waste a day of baseball.

"No you didn't, Benny," I said. I had an idea. "I know where we can get us a ball. And we don't need money, either."

I wanted to keep playing ball, and I figured it was my turn to get a new one anyway. And I remembered Bill's baseball on display in his trophy room. After all, it was only a ball. Right?

I ran home quickly. Mom was still at the airport with Bill. I was alone in the house. Creeping into Bill's room—I wasn't allowed in there—I grabbed the ball off the silver pedestal and ran. I made it back to the field in no time at all.

"I got it," I yelled as I threw our new ball to Benny.

"Cool," he answered, handing me the bat. "Your ball, your ups."

I stood at home plate. Ham, the catcher, squatted down behind me. We both waited for the pitch.

DeNunez gripped the ball and smacked it into his mitt a couple of times. Then he pitched.

Strike one. Strike two. I didn't want to strike out. I held the bat tighter and leaned in, just as I'd seen Benny do.

On the third pitch, I connected, hitting it hard. So hard, I knew it had to be a home run!

I dropped the bat and began my casual run around the

bases, enjoying the feeling of knowing I'd hit a homer. I watched the ball fly toward Benny in the outfield.

I had never seen anything so beautiful before. And I had never been so happy. The ball sailed through the cloudless sky as if it were in slow motion. All the guys stared at it, their mouths hanging open. They were admiring my great hit. I could see Benny smiling and nodding his head.

Uh-oh! Wait a minute. I just remembered the big problem with a home run in the sandlot. The ball *always* ended up in Mertle's yard! But this time, it wasn't just any ball. It was Bill's ball!

"Please catch it, please catch it," I whispered to myself, hoping against hope that Benny would leap up and catch the ball.

Benny was backing up, trying to keep an eye on the ball. I slowed down, watching the ball, too. I had been so happy only a second before. Now I was in a panic.

The ball dropped. Behind the fence. In Mertle's yard. The Beast had my ball—*Bill's* ball.

"Nice hit," called Timmy. He sounded far away. I couldn't take my eyes off the fence.

"It's outta here! Who's got the big bat now, boys?" cried Benny.

"Smalls. Smalls. Smalls." The whole gang started chanting my name. They were proud of me. I was scared to death.

"Whatsa matter with you, Smalls?" asked Ham. "You just hit a decent homer."

I ran toward the fence, grabbed it, and shook it hard.

"We gotta get that ball back!" I screamed. I felt sick to my stomach.

"Yeah, sure," said Ham.

"Good one, Smalls," said Squints. "Like, we'll all just climb over the fence and ask the Beast, real nice, 'Please can we have our ball back?'" The guys all laughed.

"You don't understand!" I yelled.

"We do, Smalls," said Benny. "Take it easy."

"No, you guys don't understand. That wasn't my ball!"

"What?" everyone seemed to ask at once.

"It belongs to my stepdad. And he's gonna kill me. See, it was a present or something. He kept it in his trophy room. I ain't even supposed to go in there. I'm dead meat!"

"Okay, Smalls, think hard," said Squints. "Where did your dad get this ball?"

"I dunno...I think he got it from some lady."

"A lady?" asked Squints.

"Yeah, she signed her name on it, too. Ruth, I think. Baby Ruth."

Now the guys looked as sick as I felt. They stared at me.

"BABY RUTH?!" they said together.

They all ran to the fence and jumped up to see over.

"Well, the Beast got it," said DeNunez.

"Yup, you're a dead man, Smalls," said Timmy. "Nice knowin' ya."

"Nice knowin' ya," said Repeat.

"What? Who is this lady?" I wanted to know. I knew I was in trouble—but these guys thought it was a lot worse!

"Holy... What did he say?" asked Ham. "I can't believe my ears."

"The Sultan of Swat," said DeNunez.

"The King of Krash," said Bertram.

"The Colossus of Clout," said Timmy and Repeat together.

"The Great Bambino!" yelled Ham.

"BABE RUTH!!" everyone said.

"Only the greatest ballplayer who ever lived," added Benny.

Uh-oh! Now I really was dead meat. So I finally found out who this Great Bambino was. What was the use? My life was over.

Ham was a chubby kid who could find the fun in just about anything.

Squints had a big crush on an "older woman."

Wendy Peffercorn was nineteen and beautiful.

We watched Squints
climb the board and walk
to the end. It was as if he
were walking the plank in
a pirate movie.

"Get outta here, kid,"
Wendy yelled. "And your
friends, too. And don't
ever come back, either!"

We'd just started the first game of the day when a bunch of Little Leaguers pulled up on their bikes.

"You bob for apples in your toilet—and you like it!"

To celebrate our baseball superiority, we went to the town carnival that night. And Bertram took out a package of "chaw" and passed it around.

We surveyed the enemy's camp. Mertle's backyard was filled with crumpled and broken toys, from beat-up kites to melted Frisbees. And, of course, the dirt craters where missing baseballs used to be.

Benny scribbled on the ball and rubbed his thumb over it. Now it just looked like a smudge. A smudge of Babe Ruth's autograph. A fake autograph.

Benny jumped and caught hold of the fence. "Please...please ...please let me make it," he muttered as he pulled himself up with all his strength.

Benny threw a shiny new baseball into the dirt. Picking it up, he rubbed the dirt in good. The ball didn't look shiny or new anymore. That was just what we wanted.

"Okay, this ain't gonna work for your stepdad," said Benny. "But it should at least fool your mom until we get the ball back—before your stepdad comes home."

"Well, we got about a week," I said. I wasn't sure about this idea that was shaping up at all. But I had no choice.

Benny pulled a pen out of his pocket. He scribbled on the ball and rubbed his thumb over it. Now it just looked like a smudge. A smudge of Babe Ruth's autograph. A fake autograph.

"I don't know ... " I started to say.

"You gotta at least put a ball back so your mom doesn't get suspicious, right?" asked Benny.

I nodded.

My mom was a clean freak. She noticed everything. And she'd sure notice Bill's ball missing. We needed to buy some time with this fake ball.

" 'Kay. This will just buy us some time."

I felt a little better when I placed the ball back on the pedestal in Bill's trophy room that evening. At least it was something. For now.

"Honey, what are you doing in here?"

I turned around and practically fell on my face. It was Mom! I was caught!

"Um, ah, just looking at Bill's—I mean, Dad's—baseball."

"You know he doesn't like you in here, Scotty."

I walked toward the door. I wanted to get as far away from the fake ball as possible. And Mom, too.

"Yeah, I know, Mom. Sorry."

"Hey, did he ever tell you about that ball? It's his prize possession, you know."

"Naw, I didn't know... I mean, I don't know nothin' about the ball... nothin' at all."

"It was signed by Babe Ruth himself ..."

I was shocked. Even my own mother knew who Babe Ruth was! I was a first-class dork!

"... the greatest baseball player ever."

"Oh, really?"

"Sure was. He got it from his dad. And know what? Maybe someday he'll give it to you!"

I really didn't think so.

We held a special meeting at the twins' tree house the next afternoon. It was like a war conference. We were plotting to get the ball from the enemy.

"Anybody got any ideas?" I asked. I hoped someone did.

"Nope, no clue," said Squints.

I looked around. The guys were scrunching their faces up and tapping their foreheads. They were trying to think hard.

"Can't we just jump the fence and grab it?" I asked.

"Remember the Toad ..." said Ham.

"Poor, poor Toad," the twins said together.

"Oh, geez. I forgot," I said. I thought for a minute.

"I know. Why don't we just go over and knock on Mertle's door? He can get it for us." I thought this was a good plan.

"You crazy, man?" Squints yelled. "Old Man Mertle is the meanest guy that ever lived! *He's* the one that sicced the Beast on Toad in the first place. Forget about it."

"Okay, okay," I said. Another bad idea shot down.

Suddenly, Squints jumped up.

"First, we gotta assess the situation," he cried.

"Yeah, right, of course. Good one, Squints," we all said, not really knowing what he was talking about. But at least it was something.

"First we survey the enemy's camp, then we note the surrounding terrain," he continued.

We were confused.

"What?" asked Ham.

"Oh, er, I just heard that on TV. I think it means check it out. Let's look out the window."

I only felt worse when we looked down on Mertle's backyard. It was filled with crumpled and broken toys, from beat-up kites to melted Frisbees. And, of course, the dirt craters where missing baseballs used to be.

I saw a huge chain. It looked as though it was moving. Then I was sure I saw a paw. Not just any old dog paw. A *monster* paw. It was pushing my ball—my Babe Ruth ball—through the dirt. The Beast knew we were watching. And he was teasing us. We had to get that ball back.

"He's darin' us to come get it," said Benny.

"Yeah, he's just waitin' for us to get close. Just like Toad," added DeNunez.

We had a moment of silence for poor Toad.

Only a minute before, no one had any ideas. Now everyone was shouting out their plans at once. It got very loud inside the tree house, with everyone yelling, arguing, and pointing. But at least we had a start.

We had only five days until Bill returned. We had to work fast. And we did.

DAY 1:

We started off simply, hoping we could get the ball back without too much damage. We didn't know what we were up against.

First, we grabbed an old broomstick from the twins' yard and went over to the fence. Ham held one end and pushed the other through the bottom of the fence. Squints was the lookout, peering through the little hole to see where the ball was.

SNAP!

Ham felt a tug. He pulled the broom out. It was nothing but a toothpick now. The Beast had snapped it in two.

Later that day, we sawed off the clothesline pole. It was heavy and it was metal. No way the Beast could eat through this.

As we stuffed it under the fence, something on the other side grabbed it. We couldn't hold on. It went under. A loud crashing sound came from beyond the fence.

CRASH!

The metal pole was thrown back over the fence. It was twisted into a pretzel. This was not going well.

DAY 2:

Bertram's idea was next. He brought an old flying-insect doll...

"I swear, it's my sister's!"

... that we would sail down into Mertle's yard. We put bubble gum on the doll's feet and attached a string.

Bombs away!

The doll landed right on the ball. The ball stuck to the gum. Slowly, we pulled the string, lifting the doll—and the ball—back toward the tree house.

CHOMP!

Too late! The Beast grabbed the doll in his mouth—whole. The string snapped. The ball fell back to the ground.

Back at our war meeting in the tree house, we knew we needed bigger weapons.

Some of the guys got their moms' vacuum cleaners. We hooked the pipes together and put Ham's catcher's mask on the end pipe. This was to secure the ball.

Together, the vacuum pipes were thirty feet long. This was enough to reach from the tree house to Mertle's yard. And we hooked them up with an extension cord to an outlet in the garage. Somehow it all worked.

Slowly, steadily, we all moved the big, wobbly pipe over the fence and toward the ball. The mask was getting closer to the ball. Closer. Closer. Got it! The ball was right at the mask.

"Okay, boys, throw the switch!" cried Squints.

On went vacuum one. Then vacuum two. Finally, vacuum three was turned on.

WHOOSH! It was very loud. But it was working. The ball was sucked from the ground and up into the catcher's mask.

"We have suction!" called Squints. "Let's pull! Pull it up!"

BANG!

Suddenly, the vacuum pipes wobbled. Big Beast teeth closed in on the end pipe. He had closed off the pipe. All the suction from the vacuum cleaners had nowhere to go— except back through the pipes. Into the tree house.

We heard a strange sound and knew it was trouble.

Shouting and screaming, we all leaped out of the tree house. All except Squints. The vacuums exploded in the tree house, sending everything flying. Squints landed next to us on the ground. His face was completely covered with dirt.

"Okay, we're going about this all wrong," he said, coughing. "What we need is to surprise the Beast. We need to build a tunnel."

DAY 3:

We got to the sandlot early the next day. With flashlights taped to our caps and shovels in hand, we dug a tunnel. With eight guys, it didn't take too long to dig a tunnel from the twins' yard to Mertle's.

"Okay, here I go," I said. I was scared to go. But I was even more scared of not getting the ball back.

With a rope tied around my waist, I crawled through the tunnel. Yeah-Yeah waited on the sandlot side of the fence to serve as a lookout. It was dark in there. I peeked up through the tunnel and could see just a little of the ground on Mertle's side of the fence. That was enough. The ball was lying near me. I reached my hand over and touched it. It felt slimy. Dog slime.

"I got it! I got it!" I yelled to the guys.

SQUIRT!

I had it. Then it squirted right out through my fingers. It rolled away. Right over to the Beast.

He looked up, roared, and started to lunge.

"Aaaaaaahhhhhh!!" I screamed. I didn't wait to see more.

"Oh, my gaw! It's huge," Yeah-Yeah hollered. "Pull him out, quick! PULL HIM OUT!"

With one big tug, I was out. I plopped onto the grass in the twins' backyard. I was sweating and scared. But Yeah-Yeah had passed out cold. You'd think he had been the one crawling through the tunnel.

The guys turned a hose on him. He woke up sputtering, "Holy geez! It's a dinosaur…it's humongous… get Smalls out! Wh-wh-where am I?"

"Yeah-Yeah, calm down, man. What'd ya see?" asked Squints.

"Oh—it was, like, dark and huge… like the world was ending and it was the devil, see, and he was coming up through the ground and—and—and." Yeah-Yeah couldn't speak straight.

"Snap out of it, Yeah-Yeah," said Ham.

Squints leaned over and slapped Yeah-Yeah good across the face.

"Thanks, I needed that," said Yeah-Yeah.

The tunnel didn't work. So we had to try something new. And we were desperate.

With Repeat's old tricycle, a block and tackle, a fishing pole, and a body harness, we made ourselves a pretty good crane. If we lowered somebody over the fence, he could just grab the ball and we'd pull him right back into the tree house. Easy.

"No way, man, I ain't doin' it!" said Yeah-Yeah.

"But you're the lightest guy here, Yeah-Yeah," said Benny.

"I can't, I can't, nothin' against you, Smalls, but ..." Yeah-Yeah said.

"Sorry, man. I guess your old man'll shoot you or somethin'," said Benny to me.

"Tough luck, kid," added DeNunez.

"It won't work, guys," said Yeah-Yeah. "I didn't hit the ball over the fence anyway!"

No one said a word. Yeah-Yeah looked around at all of us.

"Aw, okay. But when I say pull me up, you *better* pull me up!" he said. We strapped him into the harness.

Yeah-Yeah had a tin-can phone to talk to us from far away. As we lowered him over the fence, he gave us directions.

"Okay, I can see it. I'm right over it."

Ham looked at his watch and, suddenly, Yeah-Yeah was plunging fast toward the ground. Toward the Beast.

"Whoa! Hey, what the—" he screamed as he fell.

Ham grabbed the crank and pulled him back. Yeah-Yeah was now hanging over Mertle's yard.

"'Kay, tip me over a little. Hurry up, I'm gettin' the creeps," said Yeah-Yeah into the tin-can phone.

He reached over and grabbed the ball.

"I got it! Now pull me up. NOW!"

Ham pulled hard, but couldn't hold on for long.

"Help! I'm losin' him!" he cried.

"Oh, no! Help, guys, get me outta here!" screamed Yeah-Yeah, who was dangling right above the Beast.

We all jumped to help Ham crank Yeah-Yeah back up to the tree house. We could hear the low growl of the Beast and felt a tug on the line.

We pulled harder. We had to rescue Yeah-Yeah.

Finally, he came flying up through the tree-house window.

He was crying and swearing. He also smelled as if he had missed the toilet.

"Yeah-yeah, so what? You dorks. You jerks! I told you to pull me up!" said Yeah-Yeah. He was so scared, he had dirtied his pants. Now he waddled away, still swearing and muttering under his breath.

Another failure. I was beginning to think we'd never get that ball back. I was in major trouble.

DAY 4:

On the very last day before Bill was supposed to come home, I had an idea.

"Anybody got an Erector Set?" I asked the guys in the tree house.

"Is that the thing with all the gadgets and nuts 'n' bolts?" asked Squints.

"That's it!" I answered.

"Never heard of it," said Squints.

"I had one when I was a *little* kid," said Ham.

"Well, maybe I got some pieces." "I'll go have a look." "Maybe there's something in the attic." Everyone was talking at once. I had a feeling we would get a lot of parts. Even if no one would admit they played with toys!

Meeting back at the tree house later, we had plenty of Erector Set stuff. I got to work.

This was going to be the fanciest weapon yet. Wearing my own hard hat, I supervised as the guys put pieces together and built my machine. I tinkered with the tiny motors and pulleys. I guess all that time Mom said I'd "wasted" in my room was coming in handy after all.

Finally, a thirty-five-foot electric catapult stood next to Mertle's fence. It was just like the one I'd use for my marbles at home, only bigger. I sat in the tree house, steering the catapult over to the ball. Benny stood back, on the ground. He had his glove. He was ready to catch the ball as it was shot from the other side of the fence.

I scooped the ball.

"Fire," yelled Squints.

I flipped a switch and the ball went flying into the air, toward the fence.

"I got it, I got it," Benny yelled as he ran for the ball.

SMACK! CRUNCH!

The Beast! He had caught the ball in mid-air. With his huge teeth. Worse, he had landed on my Erector Set!

That was it. Our last idea. Our last chance to get the ball back. Bill would be home tomorrow morning. By tomorrow night, I would be dead meat. I was doomed.

I said good night to the guys … probably for the last time. Then I walked home.

CHAPTER 8

"**L**isten up, guys, I'm only gonna say this once," Benny said as we walked onto the sandlot. Today was the day Bill returned, and the gang was already there. They were ready to try one last time to save my ball—and my life. "I'm goin' in after the ball. And I ain't comin' out 'til I get it."

"Benny, wait!" I said. "It's not your problem. I'll catch heck for this from Bill—but I can take it. Honest. You don't have to do this!"

"Yeah, I do," Benny answered.

At that moment, we all believed him. We knew we had to let him try. But I was the only one who knew why.

Benny had knocked on my bedroom window early that morning. He woke me up. After climbing into my room, he had told me about his dream of the night before. His dream made him decide to go into Mertle's yard and get the ball. At least, he told me it was a dream. But I wasn't so sure.

Smoke and lights were shooting out of Benny's bedroom closet as he tried to sleep, he told me. Jumping up in bed, he had pressed himself flat against the wall.

"M-M-Mom... that you?"

With a loud creak, the closet door opened. All by itself!

"Who's there?"

Standing in the shadows was a shape that looked like a man. But it was weird. He looked like an old black-and-white movie on TV. He wasn't in color.

Benny had looked closer, trying to see through the smoke. "Oh, my... Holy...!"

It was the Sultan of Swat, the Great Bambino—BABE RUTH!

"Now don't go peein' your pants or anything," said the Babe. "I'm only here to help you out of a jam."

Babe Ruth, right there in Benny's room! Benny had rubbed his eyes a few times to make sure he was awake. It was hard to see, anyway, because the Babe was smoking a big old cigar. That was where all the smoke came from.

"B-b-but ... you're not, I mean you're ... "

"Dead?" asked the Babe. "Legends never die, kiddo."

"You're really him, it's really you! The King of Krash, the Great..."

"Bambino, yeah, that's me. I love all those nicknames. But enough of that. I'm here 'cause you got yourself into some kind of pickle, am I right? And we don't got much time."

"How'd you..."

"I just know, kid. A baseball with my autograph went over a fence, right? Can't get it back, right?"

"Yeah, right."

"Okay. Alls you gotta do is hop the fence and get it. Case closed. See ya later, kid."

"No, wait! You don't understand. We *can't* go over the fence."

"Why not?" The Babe had started back to the closet. He turned around and looked at Benny.

"There's a huge beast in there. A giant, King Kong–type thing that ate one kid already!"

"You don't say. Hmm. Listen, kid, everybody gets *one chance* to do something great. Lots of times people don't even know when their chance comes; most people don't take chances at all.

"Here's your big chance. Don't let it go by."

"But ..."

"Remember those cards you got the other day?"

"Yeah, five Maury Wills in one pack."

"What are the odds on that, eh?"

"About a zillion to one, I guess."

"Probably more. Point is, someone's trying to tell you something. I think you'd better listen."

"But how?"

"You got the rubba legs, am I right? Figure it out."

The Babe leaned over Benny's bed and blew a ring of smoke.

"Look, kid, you gotta follow your heart, else you'll spend the rest of your life wishing you had."

"Are you telling me I gotta *pickle* with the Beast? Like I do in a ballgame?"

"Lemme tell you something. Remember that home run I called before I even hit it?"

"Heck, yeah. That's the most famous, the greatest, unbelievable homer of all time!"

"You're right. But d'ya think I knew I'd hit it like that?"

"Sure, 'course ya did, Babe."

"Naw. In fact, all the way to first I kept telling myself, 'You lucky bum.' Think about it."

The Babe walked back into the closet. The door closed. He was gone.

Back on the sandlot, Benny laced up his new running sneakers. He looked up at the fence. He swallowed hard. He was afraid, but he was going to do it.

With an easy run, Benny jumped onto the fence. After a quick thumbs-up sign to us, he turned and plunged over the fence. He was now in Mertle's yard. With the Beast!

Benny looked around, trying to figure out where the Beast was. He didn't have to wait long.

A huge figure stood up in front of Benny. It was the Beast. He was bigger, uglier, and meaner than we thought. And here he was—the *real* thing!

He dropped something out of his mouth. It rolled over to Benny's feet. It was the ball. The Babe Ruth ball.

Benny and the Beast eyed each other. Who would get to the ball first?

Benny lunged forward. At the same time, the Beast crouched and leaped. Benny got there first. He grabbed the ball. It was covered with dog slime. The ball slipped out of Benny's hands. He grabbed it again, and this time stuck it between his teeth.

His hands were free, and he leaped toward the fence. The Beast was right behind him, snapping his sharp teeth at Benny's shoes. Benny jumped and caught hold of the fence.

"Please...please...please let me make it," he muttered as he pulled himself up with all his strength.

The Beast had reached the end of his chain. He pulled once, then twice. It broke! The Beast was no longer chained in his backyard!

"Yowwwww!" screamed Benny.

He cleared the top of the fence and came down hard.

We were ready to cheer when we noticed a huge shadow on top of the fence. It was the Beast.

The Beast was loose! And he was after Benny!

Before we had a chance to move, Benny took off.

"Ohhhhh!" we heard him yelling as he raced through the sandlot and into town.

The Beast was right on his heels.

"Let's go!" I screamed at the other guys.

"Right behind you, Smalls." "Get him guys." "Go Benny, go!" Everyone yelled as we, too, chased after Benny and the Beast.

Benny was fast. But so was the Beast. They raced through the streets of town. People on the sidewalks jumped out of their way. Trash cans spilled over as the two knocked them down. Cars were stopping in the middle of the street to watch the chase.

We weren't quite as fast. But we did follow as closely behind as possible. We sidestepped trash cans and garbage. We shouted apologies to people along the way.

Benny swerved to the right and ran down an alley. The Beast took the corner a little more sharply. He almost fell over. But he got his balance and kept on running.

Ducking into a nearby building, Benny kept going. He couldn't seem to lose the Beast. Benny had run into the Boys' Club. They were showing another *King Kong* movie— this time Kong was fighting a giant dinosaur. Benny thought he was having a much harder time than that old dinosaur.

A hundred boys turned to watch Benny run through the hall. Just as they turned their attention back to the screen...

RIIIPPPP!

The growling Beast jumped right through the movie screen. He pawed a huge hole in the middle of King Kong and landed in the aisle. Then he was out the door, still chasing Benny.

"What the—" Squints said as we entered the club.

"Where'd they go?" I asked. A hundred guys pointed to the back door. We ran.

Benny was really flying now. He ran into the pool building and out onto the deck. The pool was filled with gorgeous girls getting suntans. Benny wove in and out of lounge chairs and towels.

"Hey, get outta here, buster," yelled one of the girls.

"Whaddya think you're doin'?" yelled another.

"HEEEELLLPPP!" came a scream from the doorway. All the girls began screaming hysterically when they saw what followed Benny.

Still shrieking, the girls tried to get out of the way. Too late! They went plunging into the pool, soaking their nice hairdos. They kept screaming.

The Beast slipped and slid along the wet pool deck. But he never lost sight of Benny. And he never slowed down.

Back on the street, Benny took another turn, this time toward the Little League field.

Today was Founders' Day, a big holiday around here that celebrated the people who first built the town. And the Founders' Day game was a big one. The bleachers were packed. Benny cut through, running down the baseline. He interrupted the game.

The Beast was close behind. The game stopped. Kids and parents alike watched in surprise as the huge dog chased the boy. Just as the teams were ready to begin again, the gang and I ran through the field. We ran in the same direction as the others. We thought we were such great baseball fans, but we never even stopped to see who was winning the game!

Farther downtown, toward the park, hundreds of people were gathered for Founders' Day picnics and parades. Benny ran through the neatly set up picnic tables.

"Thanks," Benny shouted as he grabbed a Coke from someone he passed. He kept on running.

The Beast continued the chase. He didn't stop for a drink.

Suddenly, Benny was face-to-face with a huge bass drum. He swerved to one side just as the drummer began to pound. It was loud.

Zigging and zagging, Benny ran through a row of horn players and a bunch of majorettes. He rubba-legged, just like in a ballgame. Smoothly, he made it through the parade marchers. The band never missed a beat.

The Beast was not so graceful. He tore through the parade, knocking over clowns and musicians like bowling pins. Little kids were swooped up by terrified parents. Even the mayor was knocked out of his convertible. But the Beast just kept running. He was right behind Benny now. And the parade was one big mess.

"Where'd he go? What's goin' on? Where is he?" we were all asking one another. We had lost Benny back at the picnic grounds. Where did we go next?

"SANDLOT!" cried Benny, shooting by us in a rush.

"SANDLOT!" we all yelled, heading for our field.

"C'mon, I know a shortcut," said Squints. We followed Squints through an alley and a couple of backyards.

We made it to the sandlot quickly. Benny and the Beast were already there. In fact, they were headed right for us!

"Awwwwww!" everyone yelled. We scattered out of the way.

"LOOK OUT!" screamed Benny, flying by us at top speed.

The Beast's sharp teeth snapped at Benny and tore off his back pocket.

Heading straight for the fence, Benny couldn't stop. He reached the fence. Then, unbelievably, he ran *right up the side!*

Unfortunately, the Beast stayed with him. He, too, struggled up the fence.

Benny was now back behind Mertle's fence—right where he started!

We climbed up and peeked over the top. There was Benny, sitting on the ground. He held up the Babe Ruth ball.

"I got it!" he cried.

We all cheered.

Until we heard a growl. It was the Beast! Benny dropped the ball.

I turned and caught my shirt on the fence. This was it. I was doomed!

But the Beast was caught, too. His chain was tangled in the fence, and it was choking him. He was going to die if he didn't get loose. I had to help him!

"Hey, guys, over here!" I shouted. "Help me lift him. He's stuck."

I ripped my shirt and pulled free. I was scared. But as I stared at the Beast, he looked scared, too. In fact, he just looked like a big dog. The Beast whimpered.

I got him loose and, together, we fell from the fence to the ground.

Now, I was face-to-face, nose-to-nose with the Beast.

"Oh, my gaw," said Squints.

"That's it for Smalls," said Ham.

"He was a heckuva good guy," said DeNunez.

The guys slapped their hands over their eyes. They didn't want to see me get eaten by the Beast.

He opened his mouth, showing me all his huge teeth. He leaned closer. I closed my eyes. This was it, all right!

I felt something wet and warm on my face. Drippy wet. I opened one eye, then the other. The Beast had licked me! He really *was* just a dog!

I turned to the gang. Their mouths were hanging open. I flashed the thumbs-up sign.

"It's okay, guys," I said. "He's just a dog!"

I looked at his name tag. Hercules. I thought that was a good name for such a big dog. Especially one as unusual looking as he. I didn't know much about dogs, but I could see why we thought he was more of a beast than a pet. He had short, tan hair—or fur, whatever—and dark-brown ears that drooped. His face was so huge, all you could really see were teeth. But it was his size, more than anything, that had scared us all this time. Standing next to me, Hercules came right up to my shoulders. I probably could have ridden him like a horse!

He wagged his tail hard and ran through the broken fence and into his backyard. He dug around in the dirt, making a big hole.

"Willya look at that!" I cried.

We all leaned closer, looking into the hole. There were 150 baseballs lying in the dirt!

"Man, we can play forever now!" shouted Benny.

We all laughed and cheered. I stopped laughing suddenly. I remembered something.

There was one more thing left to do. And it scared us all more, even, than the Beast.

We had to bring Hercules back to mean Old Man Mertle.

CHAPTER 9

"**G**o on, Smalls," said Squints.

"We're with you, buddy," agreed Ham.

Oh, yeah, then why am I the only one steppin' up and knockin' here? I thought. I didn't say anything. But I was really nervous. Taking a deep breath, I knocked. The guys were standing behind me.

What if Old Man Mertle grabbed me and dragged me inside? What if he had an ax—or a chain saw?

The door was old. The paint was peeling and the hinges were rusted. I wondered when was the last time someone knocked on this door.

CREEEAAAKK!

"WHO'S THERE?" a voice boomed out from behind the door. It opened slowly and very loudly.

My throat was dry. I couldn't speak.

The door opened wider. There stood Old Man Mertle. Funny, he didn't look like a mean old man. He didn't look scary at all.

"What can I do for you, son?" he asked.

I looked at him for a moment. He was old, all right, but he was smiling. He had big, dark glasses on. He didn't have an ax or a chain saw. I looked again. He was blind!

"I—um, we brought your dog back," I stammered.

"Hercules?" he asked. "Now how'd he get out, I wonder?"

At the sound of his name, Hercules pulled forward and

licked Mertle's hand. He sat down and nuzzled the old man's leg. He really was a nice dog.

"Well, sir, um, Mr. Mertle, you see, it kind of happened like this ... " I started.

"We hit a baseball into your backyard," said Benny, climbing up the porch steps. "Then we tried to get it back, and ... "

"Well, shoot, boys, I would've gotten it for you," said Mertle. "Why didn't you just come on up to the door?"

THUMP!

I turned around just in time to see Squints, Yeah-Yeah, DeNunez, Timmy, Repeat, and Bertram faint. Dead away.

Jeez, after all we went through! We could have just knocked on Old Man Mertle's door!

"Thanks for bringing Hercules back to me," Mertle said. "Say, why don't you come on in. We can talk baseball."

Benny and I looked at each other. Mertle seemed okay. *And* he liked baseball. We walked into the house. After the door slammed, I could hear the guys shuffling around. Sounded like they were heading out of the yard—probably back to the sandlot.

Inside, we looked around in surprise. Mertle not only liked baseball. He *loved* it. In the middle of the living room was a huge baseball diamond. It was green felt, and had little bases, an outfield wall, and tiny little players.

"Check it out," said Benny.

"Awesome!" I agreed.

As we moved closer to the baseball diamond, we noticed something on the wall. It was a picture. It was Mertle—and *Babe Ruth!*

"You knew the Babe?" Benny asked in a whisper.

"Sure did," Mertle replied. "He knew me too, heh, heh," Mertle chuckled, taking the picture off the wall.

"They never let me and the Babe play together, but we were friends. Good friends. He was almost as great a hitter as I was." Mertle chuckled again. "But he'd a told you he was better!"

He held the picture for a moment, then handed it to us.

"To Thelonius Johnson Mertle, the second-greatest slugger I ever saw, Babe Ruth," Mertle said. He couldn't see the picture to read the autograph. But he knew what it said by heart.

"Base hit," announced a radio nearby. Just like Squints, Mertle was always tuned into a baseball game on his radio. As each play was called by the announcer, Mertle placed the players in the right position on his big diamond.

"I know baseball like I know myself," Mertle said. "And even though I can't see no more, I still play." He nodded toward the diamond. "Usually win, too," he laughed.

Benny and I smiled at each other. Old Man Mertle was all right.

"This the ball that went over my fence?" Mertle asked. "I found it in my yard."

He held up our ball. Bill's ball.

"This is an old ball—really old," he continued. "Feels like Hercules gave it a good chewing, too, eh?"

"Yes, sir," I said. The ball was a mess. It was tattered, and the seams were pulling apart. And it still had dog slime all over it. The Babe's autograph was worse than a smudge now. I couldn't even read it.

"You sound upset, son," Mertle said. "What's the matter?"

"Well, this isn't really my ball—it belongs to my stepdad. Uh, see, it was signed by Babe Ruth, and ... "

"Hmmm, yeah, I get it. Well, you know, I'm sure your dad will understand."

"I don't think so," I said. I was still doomed.

"... And Maury Wills makes his move! He's stolen second base!" the radio announcer yelled.

"Son, would you please move Wills to second for me?" Mertle asked Benny.

"Sure," said Benny as he moved the tiny figure to second base.

"That Wills!" Mertle continued. "If he steals third, that'll be a hundred stolen bases!"

"He will," said Benny. If there was one thing he knew, it was Maury Wills.

"Son, looks like you're in a heckuva pickle. Here, I'll make you a deal," said Mertle.

He got up and took something off the shelf. It was a baseball. He held it out to us.

"If you boys'll come over once a week and talk baseball with me, I'll trade balls with you right now."

Benny cleared his throat. He didn't want to hurt the old man's feelings. But what kind of trade was that?

"That sure is nice of you, Mr. Mertle," said Benny. "But, see, this ball *really* is signed by the Babe."

"Heh, heh, so's this one—and by all the rest of the 1927 Yankees," said Mertle.

I reached out for the ball as Mertle handed it to me.

"Oh, my... it really is the whole team." Benny could hardly believe his eyes.

I didn't know who any of these guys were. But as I read the names, Benny just whistled.

"Lou Gehrig ... BABE RUTH!" I read.

"They're all there," said Mertle, smiling.

"DEAL!" Benny and I said at the same time.

We laughed and shook hands with Mertle. We promised to visit him every week. We had a lot to talk about.

"Wills just captured his hundredth stolen base! It's incredible," the radio announcer screamed.

"Yes!" yelled Benny.

This was a lucky day.

"Uh-oh," I suddenly said. "My dad! He might be home!" I looked at the clock. "I gotta go! Thanks, Mr. Mertle."

"Yeah, it was nice meetin' you. We'll be by again real soon," said Benny as he ran down the steps after me.

Benny and I raced to my house. Our sneakers squeaked as we stopped at the screen door. Too late. Mom and Bill were already there. And Bill didn't look too happy.

"Just what is going on here, Scott?" he said with a growl.

"And this better be good," he added.

I took the ball from behind my back and raised it up for Bill to see. He took it. He frowned. He read the names.

"Wha ..." he started to say.

I shuffled my feet and looked at the boards on the porch. Then I looked at my mom, and at Benny. I didn't know if this would be the last time I ever saw them. I started imagining all kinds of terrible things. Would Bill like the ball? Could this ever replace the one his father gave him? Would I be grounded for the rest of my life? Would I ever play with the guys again?

Bill looked at the ball for a long time. His eyebrows puckered as they did when he had a lot on his mind.

Oh no, this is it. I thought I was a goner. I closed my eyes.

Then I heard something strange. It sounded like a chuckle. Laughter. I couldn't believe it. Who was laughing at a time like this?

I opened my eyes slowly and looked straight at Bill. His face was red. It was Bill laughing! I smiled, just a little, wondering what all of this meant.

"Well, kid, you've got spunk, that's for sure," said Bill, still laughing. "And you sure know how to get yourself out of a pickle."

I looked over at my mom. She was smiling wide, and I thought I even saw a tear in her eye. I don't remember ever seeing her that happy.

Bill ruffled my hair and said, "How 'bout a game of catch?"

After that, Bill really became "Dad" to me. He bought me a new glove. We played catch in the backyard almost every night.

Benny and the guys, we all visited Mr. Mertle once a week—sometimes more. We listened to baseball games on the radio and played them out on his diamond.

Even Hercules became part of our team. He was the biggest mascot in town.

"SAFE! SAFE! SAFE!" the umpire yelled.

"What a play! He's done it again. And the Dodgers win the pennant! Unbelievable! The Old Man stole home!" the radio announcer yelled.

At home plate, the team gathered around the runner. They patted him on the back yelling and cheering. They were all wearing Los Angeles Dodgers uniforms. They had just won the pennant and were on their way to the World Series.

In Dodger Stadium in 1993, Benny Rodriguez was one of the oldest players in pro baseball. But he was still one of the fastest guys around. And he had just scored one more time for his team.

His coach shook his hand.

"Good work, kid," he said. The two walked away. They went to the dugout. On the back of the coach's uniform was the name "Wills."

Thirty years after our sandlot team played ball every day, Benny was a hero. A professional, major-league ballplayer. His idol, Maury Wills, was now his coach.

Somehow, we had always known that Benny would go on to great things. And he did.

After that long-ago summer, we never played together again as a team. But we never forgot it.

Yeah-Yeah's parents sent him to a military school, so we didn't see him much.

The twins, Timmy and Tommy, grew up to build skyscrapers.

Ham went to college and is a doctor now.

DeNunez played ball. But he never made it to the majors.

Bertram became a hippie and we never saw him again.

Squints grew up and married the girl of his dreams—Wendy Peffercorn, the lifeguard! They bought the old drugstore in town and still own it today.

Hercules lived to be 199 years old—in people years—I heard. Anyway, he got to be really old.

And me, the shy little kid who didn't know anything about baseball . Well, that's me announcing the games. I'm one of the TV sports announcers for the Los Angeles Dodgers—Benny's team.

That summer of 1962 is still like a dream to me. Everything was larger than life. Baseball was our reason for living. Hercules was our idea of King Kong. We sandlot players were a real dream team. And even though we eventually discovered that dreams don't always come true, I think every one of us carries a part of that summer somewhere deep inside.

Sometimes, though, dreams do come true. Benny and I are still a team. Just as I dreamed when I met him. A long time ago.